W9-BWL-565

Bunny

Watch me grow!

Photographs by
Nancy Sheehan

Dutton Children's Books • New York

A Special Day

When it's time to have her babies, this mother rabbit goes inside the nesting box that has been placed inside her hutch. The box is filled with clean straw and wood shavings.

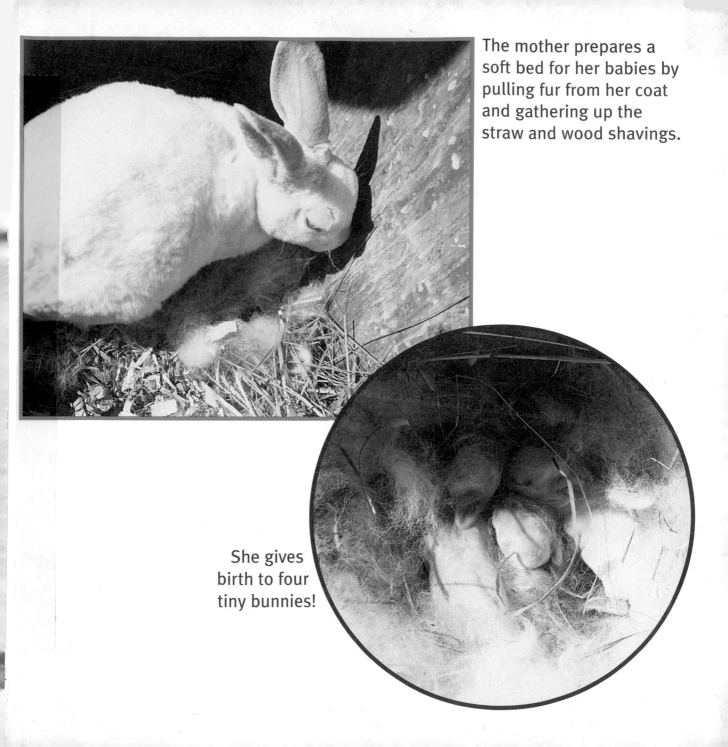

The mother prepares a soft bed for her babies by pulling fur from her coat and gathering up the straw and wood shavings.

She gives birth to four tiny bunnies!

Newborns

ewborn bunnies have no fur. Their skin is pink, and they cannot see or hear.

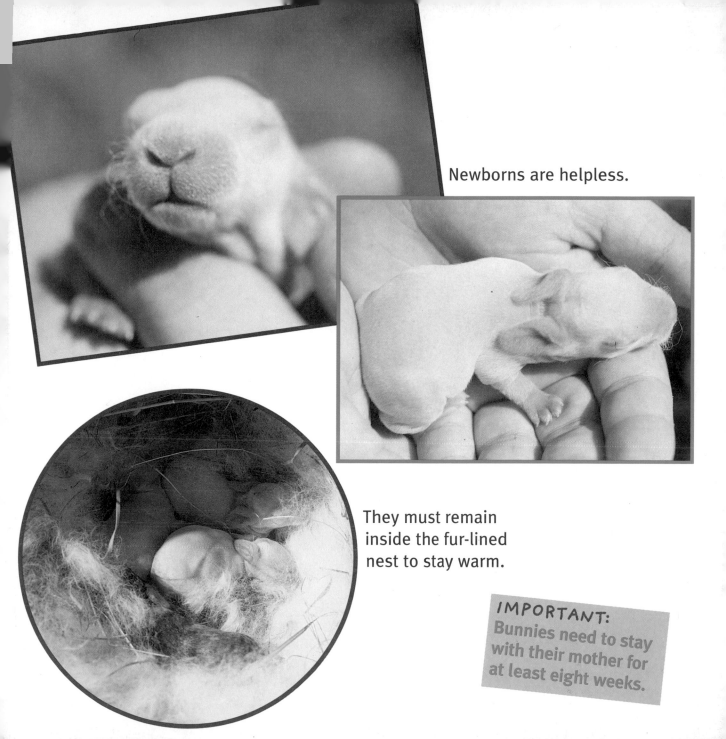

Newborns are helpless.

They must remain
inside the fur-lined
nest to stay warm.

IMPORTANT:
Bunnies need to stay
with their mother for
at least eight weeks.

Sleeping and First Steps

During the first week, baby bunnies spend most of their time sleeping in the nest. Their mother nurses them once or twice a day. Their fur begins to grow, and when they are about ten days old, their eyes open.

In about two or three weeks, the bunny is ready to take her first steps outside the nest.

She doesn't go far.

The fly on the bunny's head looks big because our bunny is very small!

She sniffs the air. There are so many new smells.

Mother's Milk

At three weeks, our bunnies have grown a lot, but they still nurse. They will continue to drink their mother's milk until they are about six weeks old.

Now that they are bigger, it's hard work getting under Mom.

Not everyone can nurse at once!

But each bunny gets a turn eventually.

Nibble, Nibble

Bunnies also begin eating solid food when they are around three weeks old. Each day they are able to eat a little more. It's important that the change from mother's milk to solid food take place gradually.

Baby bunnies begin by eating solid food out of their mother's bowl.

FACT: Bunnies need to have plenty of fresh water available for drinking.

But nursing is still essential.

Break time—sitting in the food bowl can be lots of fun!

Bigger and Braver

At four weeks, the bunny has done a lot of growing. She is bigger and stronger, and even her ears have become longer.

She ventures farther from the nest.

Family time still makes up a big part of her day.

Senses

Sight
Bunnies can't see very well close up, but they have sharp distance vision.

Taste
Bunnies are able to taste the difference between sweet, sour, bitter, and salty foods—just like humans.

Sound
Unfamiliar noises cause bunnies to be afraid. They can identify humans by the sound of their voices.

Smell
Bunnies communicate through smells and sniffing. They have a much better sense of smell than humans do.

Busy, Busy Bunnies

At five weeks, bunnies are very active. They love to dig, hop, and jump. Her sisters watch while our bunny takes a flying leap.

Bunnies often try to hide inside things, like this log. Peekaboo!

Her sisters are on the look-out as she reappears.

Tired yet? No way! This bunny is full of energy.

Rabbits Are Very Fast. They can hop 24 miles per hour for a short distance. Over long distances they move a little more slowly. If in danger, rabbits retreat quickly—sometimes first giving their enemy a powerful kick in the teeth.

This picture of a bunny from a different litter shows how the entire foot leaves the ground when it hops.

Fruits and Veggies

1 n addition to dried food, bunnies eat all kinds of greens—lettuce, tulips, cabbage, beet roots, celery, fresh grass, alfalfa, clover. Their teeth keep growing—chewing on crunchy food helps grind them down.

Hard fruits like apples and pears are good to chew on.

Raw vegetables like carrots make an excellent snack.

Rabbits have special teeth that allow them to bite through tough plants. Their front teeth are formed of hard enamel and act as sharp cutting tools.

Bunny Sounds

Some people think rabbits are silent, but that's not true. Rabbits do make noises, though they can be very hard to hear.

Growling— a short barking growl to show anger.

Teeth grinding—sometimes called "tooth purring"— occurs while the rabbit is on your lap and being petted.

Tapping or thumping— drumming hind feet on the ground to show fear.

Scrub-a-Dub-Dub

Rabbits are very clean animals. In fact, they spend more time grooming themselves than cats do! They can wash their whole bodies from the tips of their ears to the tops of their toes. Baby bunnies learn to groom from their mother.

They scrub their face with their paws.

They use their tongue like a washcloth.

They take turns grooming each other.

Rabbits like to keep the place where they live clean, too. They can be trained to use the litter box.

Fur Facts

Fur is very important because it keeps bunnies warm. Bunnies keep their baby fur until they are four months old. After that, they shed their fur twice a year—in the spring and fall.

Bunny fur is a tiny bit oily to make it waterproof. Rabbits use their teeth, tongue, and paws to keep their fur clean.

All Grown Up— Almost

At six weeks, bunnies no longer drink their mother's milk, but they still need to spend plenty of time with her. They should stay with their mother until they are at least eight weeks old.

Curious
Ears tilted forward or spread out; standing on hind legs.

Frightened
Ears tilted back; often sitting, tense and still.

Friendly
Licking and caressing is a sign of affection.

How Do You Feel?
Bunnies can't tell us how they feel, but their body language gives us some clues.

The bunnies spend longer and longer periods of time away from the nest. Their sharp senses keep them alert to possible danger.

When the bunny feels safe once more, she's ready to explore again. After all, there's a whole world out there!

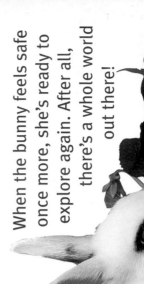

Watch Me Grow!

Two days old.

Ten days old.

Two and a half weeks old.

Five weeks old.

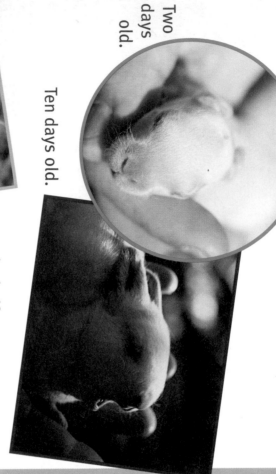

Six weeks old— see how our bunny has grown!

Discovery Communications, Inc.
John S. Hendricks, *Founder, Chairman, and Chief Executive Officer*
Judith A. McHale, *President and Chief Operating Officer*
Michela English, *President, Discovery Enterprises Worldwide*
Marjorie Kaplan, *Senior Vice President, Children's Programming and Products*

Discovery Publishing
Natalie Chapman, *Vice President, Publishing*
Rita Thievon Mullin, *Editorial Director*
Tracy Fortini, *Product Development, Discovery Channel Retail*
Heather Quinlan, *Editorial Coordinator*

Discovery Kids™, which includes Saturday and Sunday morning programming on Discovery Channel®, Discoverykids.com, and the digital showcase network, is dedicated to encouraging and empowering kids to explore the world around them.

Discovery Channel® and Discovery Kids™ are trademarks of Discovery Communications, Inc.

Published in the United States by Dutton Children's Books a division of Penguin Putnam Books for Young Readers
345 Hudson Street, New York, New York 10014
www.penguinputnam.com

Printed in USA
First Edition
ISBN 0-525-46365-8

10 9 8 7 6 5 4 3 2 1

Written by Alissa Heyman
Designed by Leah Kalotay